hand in hand

DEVOTIONS

SUSIE ROGERS, JOY MORGAN, & KAY KELLER WITH ALFRED ELLS

REMUDA *Ranch*

Unless otherwise noted, the families and individuals in this devotional are composites of the brave souls who shared their life-stories with the authors. While their names have been changed, the essence of their lives and the details of their stories have remained intact.

Hand in Hand:
Devotions for Encouraging Families Through the Pain of a Daughter with an Eating Disorder
Copyright ©2006 Remuda Ranch Center for Anorexia and Bulimia, Inc. and Susie Rogers, Joy Morgan, & Kay Keller with Alfred Ells
All rights reserved

Cover Design by Alpha Advertising
Interior Design by Pine Hill Graphics

Published by Remuda Ranch
Packaged by ACW Press
P.O. Box 110390
Nashville, TN 37222
www.acwpress.com
The views expressed or implied in this work do not necessarily reflect those of ACW Press. Ultimate design, content, and editorial accuracy of this work is the responsibility of the author(s).

Library of Congress Cataloging-in-Publication Data
(Provided by Cassidy Cataloguing Services, Inc.)

Rogers, Susie.

    Hand in hand : family devotional / Susie Rogers, Joy Morgan, & Kay Keller ; with Alfred Ells. — 1st ed. — Nashville, TN : ACW Press, 2006.

      p ; cm.
    (Series on eating disorders)

      ISBN-13: 978-1-932124-77-4
      ISBN-10: 1-932124-77-2

      1. Eating disorders in adolescence. 2. Eating disorders in adolescence—Treatment. 3. Eating disorders in adolescence—Religious aspects. 4. Parent and teenager—Religious aspects. 5. Faith. I. Morgan, Joy. II. Keller, Kay. III. Ells, Alfred. IV. Title.

RJ506.E18 R64 2006
618.92/8526—dc22   0606

Printed in the United States of America.

To the many wonderful families who have faced an eating disorder with a loved one and have begun the journey through the pain to victory.

Foreword

I'm sitting on an airplane having just spent two wonderful weeks on vacation with our daughter and her husband. A miracle has truly taken place in our family. Our daughter is happy, healthy, recently married, and about to graduate from college. Twelve years ago she was dying of anorexia and we were frantic! How could our darling ten-year-old just stop eating? Now, many years later, we have a greater understanding of the foundation of our daughter's disease and how God brought hope and healing to our family. We want to share parts of our journey to encourage other families who are struggling to understand these disorders so they may find hope.

Parents, spouses, and friends of eating-disordered women and girls have all contributed to this book. In reading each devotion, we pray you will sense our walking beside you.

Our direction and hope comes from the Lord.

Hand in Hand with Him,
Kay C. Keller

Introduction

Sixteen years isn't very old to spend each day fighting the disabling disorder called anorexia—the condition of self-starvation. While being treated for two months at a center for eating-disordered women, our daughter made the decision to overcome her anorexia. Thus began her journey toward health.

But even now her foot sometimes stumbles and the hill ahead often appears too steep. As watchful parents, we feel confused, unsupported, and very frightened. She fears that one piece of walnut or one teaspoon of margarine will cause her to gain weight. She already views her thin frame as too fat, causing us to desperately ask, "What is happening in her mind?"

Not finding easy answers, we discover that the more one tries to help (control?), the worse the situation becomes. We experience deep pain in her failures and profound joy in her victories. Everyone in the family is affected. Yet, thanks be to God, there is progress.

Remuda Ranch, the treatment center in Wickenburg, Arizona, where our daughter stayed, sent us the following words during the time she was there. For us, they were words of encouragement and we would like to share them with you.

> *Miracles do happen here. We don't make them happen, but your daughter can. It won't be easy and she must be willing to be honest, vulnerable, and open-minded. Your daughter has begun a journey that can change her life forever. She is taking this journey with the support of people who have traveled the path before her and, most importantly, with the support of God.*

We are traveling a road you may have just begun. We want to make your journey easier through these devotions. Each one is a personal story of a particular struggle we have had while on our journeys. Through a lot of trial and error, we learned to turn to God to meet our needs. We encourage you to also walk it with Him, hand in hand, as we have. Please join us.

Susie Rogers
Parent

A motel room in Wickenburg, AZ

FROM YOUR MIGHTY STOREHOUSE

Tomorrow is a harder day.
Tomorrow, I have to leave
Part of my heart in Arizona.

You understand about good-byes—
Where I've brought my child
To give her freedom to find recovery,

You sent Your Son
To be the Source of that freedom and recovery,
For her and all mankind.

My good-bye tomorrow
Will be difficult, but necessary.
Thank You for the grace to accomplish it.

Give my daughter the grace she needs to stay
And deal with the issues
She must face.

Give her courage and strength
From Your mighty storehouse.
May she feel Your awesome presence

**And hear Your applause
From heaven.**

God Cares For Us

"Casting all your anxiety on him because He cares for you."
1 Peter 5:7 (NASB)

July 25, 1995, is one day that I will never forget. Our daughter arrived at Remuda Ranch to begin sixty days of inpatient treatment for anorexia. She stood on the front steps with her little flowered suitcase by her side, trying to fight back the tears until at last the well overflowed and streamed down her hollow cheeks. I waved good-bye with an indescribable ache in my heart that could be felt deep within. My husband and I knew we had made the right decision, but it didn't make it any easier. It required her to miss school and leave behind her hamster with the babies she had hoped for all summer. Now she looked as small and vulnerable as she had that first day of kindergarten 16 years before, standing on the classroom steps and crying as I waved good-bye.

We had no more energy to help her. She had fought every attempt made at outpatient treatment. So, in spite of our fears, we took this step of faith and laid our precious package at the doorstep of this refuge. It proved to be just that—for there our daughter found nourishment for her body, healing for her soul, and confidence again in who she was.

God cared for our daughter and for us through the loving staff at Remuda Ranch. In the hills outside Wickenburg, God is working miracles.

In His Hands

Like a harpist for an hour, like a leaf suspended in the breeze, like the twinkling of sunlight on a lake, like a still expression on a Rembrandt portrait—all images of a peace my soul seeks but cannot find. Only fear is my companion when my thoughts are about my daughter.

I love you, my daughter, for my life has been entwined in yours. Like two branches on a vine are we, each growing to the top, together and yet separate. I remember the day you were born and the first moment I held you. If I could imprint words upon your heart, if I could paint a thousand canvases, if I could write a hundred books they could not even express your value. Yet you do not hear, you turn a deaf ear to my encouragement and I watch you wasting away. I told God today that I cannot be like Mary who stood at the foot of the cross and watched Jesus die. I weep, for I am powerless to save you from your determination not to eat.

Where can I find the peace my soul so desperately needs? My thoughts turn from the frailty of my daughter and myself to seek the face of the Lord. Here is where I can find the peace for which I was searching.

Dear Father, fill my mind with Your essence and engrave on my heart Your promises. Invite me to dwell in Your presence; teach me of Your omniscience for the future is like a darkened room into which I must enter, and I fear its unknown space. Hold my hand, Lord, and lead me ahead, for You alone know my tomorrow and where I should walk. The steadiness of my steps will not be from the strength I have, but from the strength of You who leads me.

> *I will instruct you and teach you in the way which you should go; I will counsel you with My eye upon you.* Psalm 32:8 (NASB)

My Daughter Is
Fearfully and Wonderfully Made

Eating disorders have many causes, one being the current body-awareness culture that impacts our daughters by putting pressure upon them to conform to unrealistic standards of outward appearance.

An interesting example of being wrongly convinced by outward appearance occurred about 1000 years before the birth of Christ. God promised the nation of Israel they could have a king. The first king, Saul, was handsome in appearance, but with a heart that became disobedient to God. The selection of the second king was different. As told in 1 Samuel 16:7, God instructed the prophet Samuel to go to Jesse's sons and He would reveal who would be king. Samuel was impressed by the magnificent stature of one son and felt certain he was the one king. But God told Samuel, *"Do not consider his appearance or his height, for I have rejected him. The Lord does not look at the things man looks at. Man looks at the outward appearance, but the Lord looks at the heart."* To the bewilderment of all those present, Samuel had to go through all seven of the sons, even the youngest one who was out in the fields, the son no one would have chosen. It was this shepherd named David who God chose and who was to become the most loved of all of Israel's political figures.

Most parents have counseled their daughters not to be caught up in appearance and not to embrace the world's misguided values. However, when it comes to appearance, the words often fall on deaf ears. True selves are put aside to conform to cultural expectations and the result can eventually be an eating disorder.

One of the greatest difficulties for me was watching my daughter become a stranger because of her eating disorder. She changed so much that she no longer fit into the society she was trying so desperately to please. In fact, for a period of several years I could not bear to look at other teenagers socializing because my daughter was so different and contrary to their world. I had hoped my daughter would be like others and that her adolescent years would be as I had pictured them—filled with dating, phone calls, parties, football games, and dances. It broke my heart to realize her high school experience would never meet my dreams for her.

Through this, God taught me a valuable lesson. I was condemning my daughter for being deceived by worldly values and yet, I had my own preconceived ideas of what she should be like based on the world's standards. I was frantic because I could not accept her differences and I could not do anything to change her. Each in our own way desired the outward appearance the world values.

I now understand God's values are different. He has no place for conformity to the world. He never intended for us all to be the same because He created us each individually. Who better understood this than David, the shepherd boy chosen to become king? He praised God in the book of Psalms for creating him as an individual.

For you created my inmost being; you knit me together in my mother's womb. I praise you because I am fearfully and wonderfully made; your works are wonderful, I know that full well. My frame was not hidden from you when I was made in the secret place. When I was woven together in the depths of the earth. Your eyes saw my unformed body. All the days ordained for me were written in your book before one of them came to be. Psalm 139:13-16

God, please help our daughters and us not to value outward appearance over inner qualities. Teach us to respect the individuality within each of us. And as You bless our uniqueness, we ask that You teach us to honor You with our heart.

You Be the Life Preserver

Caught and made a prisoner so quickly,
She didn't see it coming…My child
Though she could stop the purging
Anytime she felt like it. It seemed
Like a good tool at the time to deal
With the anger, stress, and binge eating.

In this eating disorder, her body image
Was and is so closely attached to success,
Self-worth, and self-esteem that it
Became the boat which floats here life.
Now it has become a sinking boat.
I wish I could go back and change things.
I wish I could have known how to help
Before she boarded the boat. Now
This leaking boat seeks my daughter's life.

Lord, I know there's no easy answer;
No quick fix to this problem.
Whatever it takes, make all of us willing
To work at it for as long as necessary
To succeed—to win the fight for freedom.
Help my child to not lose hope.
Keep her going, Lord. Keep her afloat
Until she finds her freedom once more
To get on with her life free of this bondage.
Lord, please be her Life Preserver
On her sinking boat
Called Bulimia.

My Temptation

Temptation: being urged, or enticed to do something immoral, sensually pleasurable, or wrong.

I arose from bed one morning with a dull headache, immediately causing me to start the day in a sour mood. To my husband's "Good morning," I grunted, "Whatever." It was too late for my morning quiet time, reading and praying, so I quickly got dressed and proceeded to the kitchen for breakfast. I noticed that the room had remained untouched by the early risers, and that my daughter was insanely performing exercises to a TV video.

I finished breakfast, packed up some materials I needed for my morning meeting, and headed for the door. Then I remembered that my daughter might have plans for the day and I would want to know. When I asked her, she impatiently answered that she canceled her plans to go to her friend's house and that she would be home when I returned. She asked what I was doing and if she could run errands with me.

"Great," I sarcastically muttered to myself. I left, forgetting to say good-bye to my husband. When I returned at noon, I prepared lunch for myself and waited for my daughter to do the same. I watched her rinse the pile of baby carrots and cherry tomatoes and arrange them on a small plate. I could feel my temper rise. Unable to stifle it, I remarked, "Is that all you are going to eat?" An angry look was my only reply. My nerves began to tingle and the muscles in my neck and arms tightened. Just then my husband came through the front door whistling and singing and asking how my day was going. He obviously knew by the look on my face and the tension in my voice. Yet he made no gesture of recognition that I was in pain and needed help. He got his own lunch and gave me an irritated glance when I slammed a drawer shut and walked out.

I spent the afternoon running errands with my daughter who was annoyed by every question I asked. I couldn't help but notice all the normal teenagers in the mall who ate ice cream cones and shopped with friends, not with their mothers. I was totally distraught by the time I got home. My husband got the full wrath of my anger and discontent when I told him I was at the end of my rope. I couldn't take any more of him or my daughter and I needed to leave town for awhile. As usual, he failed to feel my frustration and believed I magnified all my problems. I went to bed feeling absolutely invalidated and depressed, too upset to say my nightly prayers. I wondered what good they would do anyway. Tomorrow would be just the same.

Temptation. I was being tempted to live a bitter existence, blaming others for my deep disappointment and anger. Had this pattern continued, I would most likely today be chronically depressed, divorced from my husband and alienated from my daughter. The following Bible verse awakened me from my resentment.

No temptation has seized you except what is common to man. And God is faithful; he will not let you be tempted beyond what you can bear. But when you are tempted, he will also provide a way out so you can stand up under it.
1 Corinthians 10:13

I am still tempted and some days I stumble, but I made a commitment a year ago when my daughter left Remuda Ranch that I would do whatever it took on my part. Now I can better recognize when I am being tempted. So that I will not yield to my anger and bitterness, I look for the way out that God has promised. I seek refuge in my God until the temptation passes.

This Is Not a Food Issue

Lord, I ache for my daughter—
Watching her eat, then listening to her
Go through purging. God, if only I could help.
Please help me remember this is not a food issue.
But rather a distortion issue of how she sees herself.
Lord, I don't understand her feelings of inadequacy
And unworthiness. She assures me I can never
Understand, but You understand, Lord.
You are privilege to her thoughts,
You know about the war inside her head.
Even though I don't understand,
Understanding is not a prerequisite.
I love her and desire to help her with all my heart.
We, as a family, desire to do whatever it takes
To be allowed to travel the **Highway to Wellness**
With our beloved daughter.
Help us learn to depend totally upon You
For strength and encouragement
That we might encourage one another.
We want to help You produce hope in each other
As we learn to face tomorrow by changing today.
Yesterday is over and done.
Clear us of all feelings of defeat and blame
By the blood of Your Son, Jesus.
Journey with us, Lord,
For we dare not travel alone.
We need Your guidance to stay on the road
And Your strength to keep pressing onward.
We have a destination in mind, Lord.
It's that beautiful place of rest
Found in the center of Your will.

Beyond My Comprehension

One evening I collapsed after a lengthy and emotional session of pleading with my daughter not to kill herself through starvation. I sobbed helplessly, all the strength having been drained from my body; every muscle too exhausted for any purpose other than lying lifelessly on the sofa. "Lord, where are You? How do I embrace Your power to be victorious? Please come to my aid," I prayed in desperation.

I often feel I am really too weak to stop the eating disorder's attack on our family. It seems to be more powerful than all of us combined, and we are destined to stand by and watch this assailant wipe out our serenity.

But that night God listened with love and mercy. He gave me strength and hope in the midst of a dark and lonely night. I felt His strong arms envelop me and lift me up, His hands caressing my wet face, and His words soothing my aching heart. The touch was from my husband, but it was God's love that flowed through that touch and provided for my need at that moment.

As parents we must remember the truth that comes from His Word. We can cling to it when we are hurting, depleted, and hopeless.

I can do everything through him who gives me strength.
Philippians 4:13

What is impossible with men is possible with God. Luke 18:27

I am learning that it is not my strength that wins the battles, but God's strength. He enables me to rise above the trials and be the wife and mother I need to be. I now believe in a God who is not restricted to human capabilities and comprehension, but is bigger and more powerful than anything I encounter.

Discipline—Consequence of Disobedience

No discipline seems pleasant at the time, but painful. Later on, however, it produces a harvest of righteousness and peace for those who have been trained by it. Hebrews 12:11

We frequently interfered with the consequences our children deserved. My "busyness" often kept me from being an active dad. I left most of the child raising to my wife and often told her not to worry about the children's behavior since "they are just children." She had always found it extremely difficult to witness our children in pain. To avoid their discomfort, she gave counsel and warnings instead of consequences. We both overprotected them in the hope they would heed advice and be spared unpleasant consequences.

The results were two children who grew afraid of making mistakes and taking risks. They rarely experienced the self-confidence that arises from independence, and they lacked personal responsibility built from the need to solve one's own problems. I am convinced that when a children are spared the consequences of bad decisions, they will not learn the important truth that poor choices result in consequences. This could be the reason our daughter can't seem to grasp the notion that her anorexia might cost her life. If only we had let consequences be fully experienced earlier in our children's lives when the results were less serious than what they are now.

We are learning to allow consequences to occur by being willing to tolerate short-term pain for long-term gain. Lord, give us strength to face our fears, not only for our sake but the children's as well.

Letting Go

He said, "Take now your son, your only son, whom you love, Isaac, and go to the land of Moriah, and offer him there as a burnt offering on one of the mountains of which I will tell you." Genesis 22:2 (NASB)

Her therapist tells me I need to "let go"! What does that mean? How does a person do such a thing as "surrender her to the Lord"? How can I let go of her when my entire life and emotions are linked to whether my daughter eats or not. The roots are so deep. I believe if I cut those roots, she will die. I feel as though she, and her struggle with anorexia, possess me. If I do let go, does it mean I'm "giving up"?

Abraham struggled with letting go of his son Isaac—a true miracle, a child of the promise, a gift from God. I am sure he spent agonizing time in prayer before he made up his mind to sacrifice his son as God had directed him to do. Yet Abraham put the gift before the Giver. God had to cut the roots of Abraham's possessiveness in order to have first place in Abraham's heart. God removed Isaac from the temple of Abraham's heart so that He might reign unchallenged there. Abraham was willing to give all and, in the end, preserved everything. Isaac lived and went on to fulfill the promise of God. Because of Abraham's obedience in this difficult situation, God blessed Abraham and all his descendants.

A.W. Tozer, in *The Pursuit of God*, wrote a chapter on the blessedness of possessing nothing. This passage reflected his desperate struggle to turn his only daughter over to God. His prayer at the end of that chapter cut through the root of my own struggle with surrendering my daughter to the Lord.

I cannot part with her without inward bleeding, and I do not try to hide from thee the terror of the parting. I come trembling but I do come....Please root from my heart all those things which I have cherished so long and which have become a very part of my living self, so that thou mayest enter and dwell there without rival.[1]

When a person lets go or surrenders, there will be much pain and fear as the roots are severed and transplanted by God. We will truly need the help of One who understands what sacrificing or letting go of His Son is all about!

1. Tozer, A.W. (1982,1993) Pursuit of God. Camp Hill, PA: Christian Publications, Inc.

Help Me Wait On You

Wait for the LORD; be strong and take heart and wait for the LORD. Psalm 27:14

It seems every time I turn around, I am back to being my daughter's nurse. I envy my friends who do not have to cope with this. My daughter and I always arrive at her being functionally dependent on me. I do not know if we realize this cycle is happening or if we just arrive at the same place each time. We have a destructive pattern that we cannot seem to break. If her weight gets low, I panic because I do not want her to die. All of my emotional, spiritual, and physical energy goes into helping her gain weight. She shuts me out at every road of her life except taking care of her physically. Maybe I need the cycle as much as my daughter does. I know I cannot fix this, but Lord, why don't You? I know your Word says to wait on You, but...

How can I wait when everything inside says do something?

How can I wait when all seems so hopeless?

How can I wait when she may die?

How can I wait when our lives are totally out of control?

Have I become a part of the problem?

I guess the answer really has to do with letting go of being my "savior" image and trusting You, Lord. I desire to do that, but it is so very hard when I see my daughter teetering between life and death. *Please help me, Lord* to understand that there is no quick fix to her pain and You are in control.

Yet those who wait for the LORD will gain new strength; they will mount up with wings like eagles, they will run and not get tired, they will walk and not become weary. Isaiah 40:31

A Joy Found in Letting Go

Lord,
As a parent, how can I know
When to give up, cease struggling,
And just let go?
I thought because I had done it once,
I was through the painful part.
Then I got sucked in again because
My child needed me.
Now it's a repeat of the past,
Only this time, it hurts more.
Will there be another time in the future
When it will hurt even more than now?
I want to withdraw, protect myself
From all the hurt and rejection.
I don't want to consider the possible pain
Of another time down the road.
Where do I go from here, Lord?

Keep trusting Me, your Lord and Savior.
Allow Me to heal the hurt.
Stay in My Word, remain faithful
To My House of Worship,
Faithful in prayer.
Think on good things,
Love others, allow them to love you,
Allow yourself to feel My love
In all that surrounds you.
I can turn your sorrow to…
A JOY found in letting go.

God Has a Plan for Me

I absolutely love the feeling of caring for others. Whether it is in tending to a baby pet, a sick patient, a dejected friend, or a growing child, I feel satisfied, fulfilled, and needed. But sometimes a pet cannot be purchased, the patient gets well, the friend feels better, or the child grows up. Where is my significance now? What is there to replace the void so I can gracefully let go of my need and yet feel fulfilled?

I had to come to terms with this question: Could I truly disengage myself from being needed? As the parent of two adolescents, I knew I would always be a mother. I wanted a future, however, that helped me be less dependent, but not feel lonely and useless. My relationship with my daughter presented the biggest challenge of letting go because she appeared so needy with her anorexia. However, her therapist told me that she needed to assume personal responsibility, and this couldn't happen as long as I was overly involved in her life. This was very difficult for someone who for the past twenty years had been fulfilling her every need, unhealthy as it was. I cried out to God and His answer from the book of Jeremiah gave me hope.

> For I know the plans I have for you, declares the LORD, plans to prosper you and not to harm you, plans to give you hope and a future. Then you will call upon me and come and pray to me, and I will listen to you. You will seek me and find me when you seek me with all your heart. Jeremiah 29:11-13

My fear of letting go has diminished now that I know God will illuminate a new path for me to define my individuality and my uniqueness.

Confront, Do Not Nag

It is better to live in a corner of the roof than in a house shared with a contentious woman. Proverbs 21:9

When I read that "it is better to live in a corner of a roof" than it is to live "in a house...with a contentious woman," I get guilt pangs. I know that picking and nagging at my family is not healthy. When I do it, I am beginning to realize it is a sign to me that something inside is not right. That means I need to take the time to identify and confront the real problem.

For example, the other day I was trying to get hold of my husband. I called his office, his pager, and his cell phone and received no response. This was not an extremely important message, but it seemed to get more urgent as the moments passed. By the time I reached him, I was angry. With righteous indignation I fumed, "I'm glad this wasn't an emergency!" As I heard myself talking, I realized I needed some time alone before I said another word. As I thought about the situation and prayed for clarity, God showed me that my frustration was not about this *single* instance of not reaching my husband. It was about a month of poor communication. Instead of recognizing my growing discomfort with our relationship and confronting this in a timely fashion, I allowed a circumstance to wield destruction in our relationship. I reacted as a contentious woman.

I do this also with my daughter. Little things start building as she begins to pick at her food again, and to isolate through not talking and to manipulate. If I addressed each one of these events, I would be nagging and controlling. But if I let it go, I set myself up for exploding the next time it happens, leading to a destructive pattern in our relationship. To make matters worse, confronting my daughter is not easy. She is comfortable being separate. I am only comfortable being connected. So what should I do? If I do not change, I may destroy both of us.

The answer, in part, must come from my willingness to be less connected to her. It is my need to know everything that is going on inside of her that drives me to nag. I worry about her and want to help her change. Not nagging is difficult when she is so sick. But now I ask her direct questions like, "Do you want to discuss this?" If she says nothing or "no," I may make another statement, such as, "This is a very important issue. Please consider sharing it with someone." And then I let it go. I ask God to do a work in her heart and to give me the strength to not nag. I have done what I can do for the moment. I cannot change her or control her life. Only God can.

My Daughter's Needs

My daughter is hurting today, Lord.
Her pain is mine as You know. Protect her
In these attacks from the unseen enemy.
Teach her to depend upon You. Guide her
In the way she needs to go. Help me, Lord,
To recognize when words of encouragement
And love are needed more than anything else.
Transform my love into whatever she needs
At any given moment by helping me to discern
How best I can help her, yet still manage
To instill self-reliance and independence
Within her. Give both of us grace to hold
Each other accountable in whatever way
We are able to help one another. Make me
Sensitive to her willingness or unwillingness
To hear what I feel or believe about something.
Give me courage and boldness to be firm when
I need to be. Help her to be sensitive to my needs
That she not lose sight of how love is born
Out of giving. Show me, Lord, the fine line
You've drawn beyond which I should not go.
A line which says,
**Beyond this point, your child must rely
Upon Me and on herself to trust in Me.**
Never allow me to interfere, Lord,
In what You have waiting for her.
May I free my child to become all
You would have her to be, that in the end
We will love one another and You
More than ever before.

Old Dreams and New Wineskins

When our daughter was five years old, she was such a cute little girl, especially when I dressed her in pink with bows in her hair. She was a world of dreams to us. With her talents, her ingenuity, and her ambition, we envisioned a future filled with promise. Deeply devoted to her and valuing her above our own lives, we committed to being the very best parents we could be. We were full of expectation that she would, in time, be among the very best young ladies.

But at some point along the passage to womanhood she took a wrong turn, traveling down a hideous, abusive and dangerous road to death. She took the path of an eating disorder.

It's true that at first I tried, like so many others, to assure myself that there wasn't any major problem with the turn she's taken. These peculiar and compulsive things she was doing were only a phase. But eventually I couldn't rationalize them away anymore. In a panicked state I doubled my efforts to help. It was futile. She turned from me and shut me out of her life. My energy, like life-giving fuel, drained slowly out and disillusionment became my oppressor. "If only things would change …if only God would change this," I thought. Inwardly I doubted that God listened or cared. How could He care and love and allow this to happen to all of us when we only worked for good?

Have your dreams died? Mine did when I realized my efforts weren't working and God wasn't answering my prayers the way I wanted them answered. At this stage I think we all grieve—we mourn over the loss of something important to us. We first deny, then we work hard to overcome, and finally we become disillusioned, angry, and miserable. The tears don't easily stop.

Then a pivotal point arrives, a point at which we can make a decision of recommitment to go on or a decision to stay stuck in the joyless place from which we came. The decision we make hinges on whether or not we want to get our needs met by adhering to the old practices of effort and more effort, or in a new way, by examining the principles of God as they apply to our needs. If the decision is made to turn to God for our needs to be met—not in our way, but in His way—then we move forward with renewed commitment to the final stages of grieving—new hope and acceptance.

Matthew 9:16-17 is a parable—a story Jesus tells His disciples in answer to their questions as to why He does not fast like the Pharisees do in observance of the Jewish law. Listen to His words:

> *No one sews a patch of unshrunk cloth on an old garment, for the patch will pull away from the garment, making the tear worse. Neither do men pour new wine into old wineskins. If they do, the skins will burst, the wine will run out and the wineskins will be ruined. No, they pour new wine into new wineskins, and both are preserved.*

Jesus used the analogy of the wineskins because in His day goatskins were used to hold wine. As the fresh grape juice fermented, the wine would expand, and the new wineskin would stretch. But if an old skin had been used, it would have been already stretched and would break with the new wine. Jesus brings a newness that cannot be confined within the old forms. Our problems cannot be handled in the old ways; neither can our dreams be what they once were. Don't be afraid of change, of letting go of the old and allowing God to create something new in your life.

My Dream

I have a dream
And in my dream,
I see my daughter
Whole again.
I see her
Happy and enjoying life.

I look at her face
And see the face
Of a young woman
Who knows herself
To be worthy
Of love because
She has found
The Source of all love
And He has proven
Beyond a shadow of a doubt
That His love
Brings self-love,
Self-respect,
And contentment.
Life is exciting
And full of adventure,
Service, and peace
Because my child…
Is whole again.

One Mother's Look at the Past

Being a mother was a cherished role in my life. At this time in my life it is also a painful reflection. My hindsight has become 20/20, and my newly acquired knowledge has rendered my life a bit less comfortable, but much more real.

During my child-rearing years, my daughters' sweet dependency on me filled the gap of being alone in my marriage. It was far easier to devote all my energies toward them and their activities than it was to face the hopelessness of my marriage relationship. I fostered their dependency by being a "hovering Mom." I enforced limits on their freedom—limits of not only what they did (which is a good thing) but limiting them on who they were (which isn't good). I tried to keep my children from thinking and feeling differently than I did. I didn't realize how important it was to encourage individuality and separateness in conjunction with the much-needed connectedness. I am not sure if I would have had the confidence to do this back then even if I had known. I look back at my mothering and see how fearful and controlling I was. My daughter describes me as always looking over her shoulder.

Fortunately, God gave me the courage to revisit my past and taught me how to do it differently. I now realize my children and my husband aren't just mine. They aren't trophies I should cling to. They are treasures God created. It is no wonder our daughter became anorexic; she had no freedom to be who she was designed to be! The following verse has taken on new meaning for me. I have begun trusting God for their lives and mine.

…being confident of this, that he who began a good work in you will carry it on to completion until the day of Christ Jesus. Philippians 1:6

The Baggage I Carry

God, it's hard and it hurts
To have to look into my life
And see the hidden things
I carry concealed from the world.
I don't like reliving old hurts
Or examining old wounds,
But in my willingness to help my child,
I am willing to do what hurts.

I will accept the pain,
Operate on old memories—
Seemingly without anesthesia—
If in the end, I can help my child.
My **old baggage** has affected not only myself,
But all those who live with me
Including the innocent children I have raised.
Whatever there is in my past, Lord,
Make me willing to acknowledge it
In all honesty and humility.

I cannot help my child
Until I first help myself.
In fact, the only way I can
Contribute to my child's wellness
And victory over this eating disorder,
Is to first deal with the **baggage** I carry
In my own life. Please help me to be
Honest with myself and honest with You,
That in gaining peace for myself,
I can help gain it for my child.

Bless Me, O Lord

When my children were babies, I asked a lot of questions of others. When they were in elementary school, my friends and I discussed our mother roles, usually arriving at solutions and answers by ourselves. Now that they are teenagers, I never seem to have the answers. Nor does anyone else. In fact I am more likely to know better what *not* to do. For instance, don't overprotect, communicate poorly, or invade personal boundaries.

When I feel I have failed as a parent, I remember the words of the Lord spoken through the prophet Joel. He wrote about the massive locust plague and severe drought as punishment for the disobedience of Israel and Judah. Joel emphasized repentance, but he also prophesied that restoration and blessing would follow and shame would be lifted.

> *I will repay you for the years the locusts have eaten—the great locust and the young locust, the other locusts and the locust swarm—my great army that I sent among you. You will have plenty to eat, until you are full, and you will praise the name of the LORD your God, who has worked wonders for you; never again will my people be shamed. Then you will know that I am in Israel, that I am the LORD your God, and that there is no other; never again will my people be shamed.*
> Joel 2:25

I have often asked for this same promise made by the Lord to His people to be given to me as well.

Love Displaces Fear

There is no fear in love. But perfect love drives out fear.
1 John 4:18

An eating disorder is a life-threatening problem. Its presence in the life of someone we love causes worry and anxiety. We fear for ourselves, our family and for our daughters. Fear is a very strong emotion. Webster's dictionary defines it as "a feeling of anxiety or apprehension caused by the nearness or presence of danger."

When I examined my reactions to my daughter's eating disorder I found fear was the driving force behind much of what I did. Some of the thoughts that triggered my anxiety were:,

- She won't take responsibility for her own health and will continue to deteriorate.
- I won't know what to do to take care of her, and I may do the wrong thing.
- My spouse won't work on his/her problems and we will be in constant friction.
- I won't be able to get the right professional help for her and/or I may not be able to pay for it.
- She will ruin her life and mine.
- I will never be free from having to deal with this.
- I will have to live with my sorrow for a long time, maybe forever.

The Bible has a lot to say about fear. First, it is used as the word to describe the respect we should have for God. In this case, it is desirable. It is written, *"the fear of the LORD is the beginning of wisdom"* (Psalm 111:10), and *"Blessed is the man who fears the LORD"* (Psalm 112:1).

A second use of the word in the Bible, however, refers to the troubled state of mind caused by the unhealthy, unproductive fear of what might happen. According to the Scripture, this kind of fear is unwarranted for it is written, *"I will fear no evil"* (Psalm 23:4), *"Whom shall I fear?"* (Psalm 27:1), and *"Be strong, do not fear"* (Isaiah 35:4).

Until recently, these verses meant little to me because I had set the recovery of my daughter as my obsession in life. When she didn't quickly improve, I could not be anything but anxious. So I lived in fear and worry until my focus finally changed. Matthew 6:26-27 says, *"Look at the birds of the air; they do not sow or reap or store away in barns, and yet your heavenly Father feeds them. Are you not much more valuable than they? Who of you by worrying can add a single hour to his life."* Isaiah 41:10 also states, *"So do not fear, for I am with you; do not be dismayed, for I am your God. I will strengthen you and help you; I will uphold you with my righteous right hand."*

How beautiful is the image painted by these verses of God's loving care for us. I took hold of these truths. I believe in them, and recall them again and again, especially when I catch myself worrying. Now my reactions are governed by these words of love and care from Philippians 4:6-7. *"Do not be anxious about anything, but in everything, by prayer and petition, with thanksgiving, present your requests to God. And the peace of God, which transcends all understanding, will guard your hearts and your minds in Christ Jesus."*

Eating Disorders Take Prisoners

Made captive before one realizes
That slavery is on its way—
This is how it feels to have
An eating disorder. Awareness
Of the pain this news will bring
To loved ones is another guilty burden
Added to the shoulders of the Sufferer.
Once the secret is out, there is more
Than one Prisoner, for as with
So many other addictions,
The whole Family suffers the pain.

Lord, I want my daughter to recognize
That we hurt with her in this eating disorder;
Yet I do not want her to feel overly burdened
With the knowledge of our pain. This monster
Is such a big, overwhelming problem that
It will take all of our combined resources for
The fight to overcome it. No one should have
To fight alone, Lord. Join us together as one great
ARMY, united behind a great CAUSE—that of seeing
VICTORY gained over this bondage by our loved one.
May she find freedom to live again.
Use the entire process to grow us as individuals
And as a family who pulls together in adversity.
May we each be given insight as to where
Our responsibilities lie and may we be
Courageous and accountable to ourselves,
One another, and You. May good things come
From this experience, not the least of which is
Learning to depend more upon You.

Refined As Silver

*Praise our God, O peoples, let the sound of his praise be
heard; he has preserved our lives and kept our feet from slip-
ping. For you, O God, tested us; you refined us like silver.*
Psalm 66:8-10

I was talking with a friend recently whose brother was in jail due to
repeated drunk driving charges. She relayed to me a story of how
their mother is grieving over the harsh jail treatment and is writing
a letter to the judge pleading for his mercy.

Whenever I hear a story or read news coverage of the response
of a convicted criminal's mother, I am always interested. Usually the
mother has some excuse why her son (or daughter) could not be
guilty because he was such a sweet and good-natured child.
Typically Mom also thinks the judge should be lenient in his sen-
tence. It surprises me to think that one's character could be so mis-
interpreted by his mother or that she would cover up his faults. Of
course she feels that the punishment should be less harsh.

Actually, I should not be shocked at this kind of maternal reaction because I was guilty of this with my anorexic daughter. After
doing so much to aid in her treatment, she continued on her path of
disordered eating. In the beginning I was no different from the mothers mentioned above, in that my motivation was always to spare her
from the pain of her own consequences. I allowed her to manipulate
me, I gave in to her demands, and I arranged my schedule to meet her
needs. I remember times when my husband and I made rules that she
found too difficult to obey, so I pressured my husband into changing
them—to make them more lenient. I constantly ran interference
between her choices and the unpleasant results.

After year upon year of futile attempts to convince her to
improve, I finally came to the end of my efforts. I grew so weary

from all the hours I spent helping her and running interference, that I became numb inside. I stopped caring whether or not she felt the hardships from her anorexia. I wasn't sure why I felt so numb and I felt somewhat guilty for wanting to leave her to her own consequences. I prayed that God would help me to regain my interest in her problem so that I would not miss any responsibility I might still have.

Just recently God answered that prayer through an unexpected insight. I realized that I have cared more about her comfort than her character. My attitude towards my daughter has been wrong. I learned that need to step back from comforting and protecting her in order to let God do a much-needed work inside her. I have not lost my love and concern for my daughter just because I am allowing the difficult and uncomfortable outcomes to occur. Rather, I am being refined into a healthier parent, who refuses to run interference anymore between my daughter and God's loving discipline. I am pleased to be aware of this change in me. It shows that God is not only refining her but me as well.

If I said I liked the pain of refinement, I would be lying. God often needs to refine us through intense conditions. As a silversmith applies heat to silver to make the impurities surface for removal, God allows us to endure difficulties so He can refine our character by removing impurities.

How unfortunate when a mother fails to recognize that discipline for disobedience is not bad, but is a necessary refining process.

Beyond the Door Marked Helplessness

Lord, it's so tempting
In praying for my child
To ask only for the best
For her life, and in asking
For the **best** my mind
Imagines bountiful blessings
And a life without pain
Or sorrow or suffering.

Although this is my wish
For her, I know
Life comes with the bad
As well as the good.
It takes both to grow us
To be the persons You would
Have us become in You.

We would have no need of God
If we had no needs at all;
So in the loving wisdom
With which You see into our hearts,
I ask that You work in the life
Of my child, teaching her
What You taught me so long ago—

Beyond the door marked **Helplessness**
Is the stairway which leads to You.

Tough Love

For you, oh God, tested us; you refined us like silver.
Psalm 66:10

I define tough love as the action of maintaining a firm stance on certain decisions that could result in the denial of major privileges for the offender. For a child the major privileges could include things such as living in the parents' home, financial support, or possession of a vehicle. Hopefully, discipline never has to get to the point that these extreme measures have to be taken.

However, in our family the time arrived when I felt that all attempts at channeling our daughter toward a healthy life away from anorexia had failed. Nothing seemed important enough to her to instigate a change in her behavior. In our hearts, we felt that she needed to experience the consequences of her behavior without our safety net. We wanted her to experience God, to be tested by Him, and to be a better person when it was done. We based our judgment on the experiences of two of our friends who, years earlier, had chosen the same course of action with their teenager and had encountered positive results.

It took a year before my wife and I could reach the point where we felt we could administer tough love and not weaken under pressure. Our rule would be that financial support would be contingent on her commitment to a recovery program. We made it clear that we were not asking for perfection, only compliance to attend the meetings she and her therapist established and to work toward achieving a "safe" weight. Our daughter was still in control because she didn't have to obey us. After all, she was 18 and able to choose her own life. Although the ending to our story has yet to be written, we feel confident with our judgment and she has made progress.

I am learning that tough love is very difficult for me. It is not my natural inclination. I must pray for God's wisdom concerning tough love. Should I feel that God is telling me "yes," then I must be courageous to obey. The bottom line is that I need to be more concerned with the character of my child than with her comfort.

The Loneliness of Self-Pity

There are times I wake up in the morning and a creeping ugliness comes over me. I look in the mirror and see bags under my eyes. The years of sadness have certainly taken their toll. I walk to the kitchen wishing this day had never begun. I would love to be able to talk to my husband about how miserable I feel, but he has an early morning meeting. I call one of my daughters hoping just the sound of her voice might cheer me. She is already gone for the day. Today I feel so alone in my misery. Where do I turn? I need someone to listen and understand. My friends and family are weary from my troubles. I hate what my life has become—mostly filled with worry and sadness over my daughter's eating disorder. Where is the joy, Lord?

Then I grab the Bible as a last resort before I sink into my own mire of self-pity. I read, "*This is My commandment, that you love one another.*" John 15:12 (NASB)

At first I am angry. I think, "It is because of my love for my daughter that I am so hurt." But then I realize that I want to love and be loved without paying the price of love. To love is to be vulnerable. This means that I must risk being wounded. To love is to take risks, to expose our hearts. Sometimes we get hurt and disappointed. But we must choose to love in spite of the pain. Otherwise, the worst in us will win. We will become self-centered and filled with self-pity. We must choose to keep loving that daughter or spouse or sister or friend. It is Christ-like and is better than locking our heart in a coffin of self-centeredness.

Speak The Truth In Love

Speaking the truth in love, we will in all things grow up into Him who is the Head, that is, Christ. From him the whole body, joined and held together by every supporting ligament, grows and builds itself up in love, as each part does its work.
Ephesians 4:15-16

We open our mouths and words come out. We animate our faces. We gesture with our hands. We move our body in narration. In doing all of these things, we express our thoughts and ideas to another person; in other words, we communicate. But do we always share our true thoughts or feelings or have certain events in our life conceivably altered our willingness to disclose the truth? When we communicate, the dysfunction of both the speaker and the receiver usually produce communication problems. Resolving this problem involves learning to express feelings, to speak directly to the person involved, to state opinions without attaching blame, and to establish reasonable boundaries of privacy.

At Remuda Ranch, our family learned an important process of conflict resolution called "Truth in Love." During these sessions, the families of all the residents took turns communicating together for the purpose of considering past and present problems. The presiding counselors facilitated the discussions to ensure respect prevailed. Since then, our family has continued the practice of gathering once a week to discuss wounds, offer amends, or make decisions. The success of the meeting depends on the consideration of all involved and adherence to certain rules of engagement.

Our family has made much progress since the early days of conflict, but we still have much to learn. If we can keep in mind that relationships are more important than getting our own way, we tend to think before we open our mouths. Proverbs 15:1 wisely says, "A *gentle answer turns away wrath, but a harsh word stirs up anger."* And Proverbs 16:24 states that *"Pleasant words are like a honeycomb, sweet to the soul and healing to the bones."* Pleasant words create an intimacy in the expression of thoughts and ideas. Sharing, encouraging, and supporting each other verbally forms a bridge between two hearts that will remain throughout eternity.

Self-Control

"Nibble, nibble, nibble" went my daughter's teeth all around the tiny carrot she was holding in her hand. I felt like I was going to scream, "I can't stand it any longer! If I see one more tiny carrot, one more apple sliced into a hundred pieces, or one more fat-free cracker broken into morsels on your plate, I know I will have a nervous breakdown!"

Every parent of an anorexic daughter can relate to what I am saying. Day after day, we endure the ordeal of watching them ritualistically eat rabbit food at a pace that would make an elderly man without teeth appear speedy. We feel like we are being held hostage in our homes—the place we should be able to find refuge from a stressful world. Yet here we find tension. We can't fix the problem; we can't cope with it, and worse yet, we can't escape from it.

Living with someone who slowly rubs away on our sanity is like hearing a dripping faucet while lying in bed at night; the more we try to ignore it the more it occupies our thoughts. I can't tell you how many times I have come to the end of my patience and said words I later regretted. Many times I have had to literally leave our house because I can no longer tolerate seeing evidence of her eating disorder. Many nights my husband and I chose to eat in front of the TV because we are so tired of watching her strange eating habits. These methods of coping with a miserable predicament temporarily divert our frustration, but they don't replace it with peace. In my search for help I found an answer in 1 Peter 4:7.

The end of all things is near. Therefore be clear minded and self-controlled so that you can pray.

This letter was most likely written during the time of Nero's reign. Christians were being persecuted, and they needed direction on how to live for God amidst the painful trials. Peter tells the Christians that in anticipation of the end times, they should exhibit three behaviors: clear minded, use self-control, and pray.

Believers should be characterized as making reasonable, wise decisions with a clearly defined purpose in life in view of eternity. They should control themselves to behave in line with these decisions because doing so will enhance their ability to pray accordingly. I applied this advice to my situation.

For example, I now relate to my daughter based on what I believe to be the will of God for her and all of us. I now work on being self-controlled so that I behave according to what I have already predetermined to be the best action. I try to respond rather than react. Most importantly, I cover it all with consistent prayer for wisdom. Since I have begun praying for God's will and self-control, I have found that I have increased patience when I relate to my daughter. I now know it is possible to have peace even in the midst of my daughter's eating disorder.

Obedience Ensures the Ending

Shadrach, Meshach, and Abednego were three courageous men who did what was right in spite of their fears. Their story is told in the book of Daniel, chapter 3. King Nebuchadnezzar made a golden image and ordered everyone in his kingdom to bow down to it whenever the "multitude of all instruments" was sounded. Failure to do so would result in a gruesome death inside a fiery furnace! These three young men knew they could not worship a golden idol. Their faith in God and in His decree that there should be no idols before Him caused them to disobey the king's orders. News of their refusal reached the throne of the king. In a furious rage, King Nebuchadnezzar ordered them thrown to a burning death. The plan proceeded as ordered until God interceded. When the king looked into the burning furnace, he saw not only the three men surviving the fire unharmed, but a fourth figure in the fire as well. An angel from God protected them and prevented the assumed tragic end.

The story is an illustration of personal obedience to God in the face of fearful consequences. I am in the same predicament. I am attempting to follow my husband's wisdom in dealing with our daughter and her anorexic condition, instead of reacting like I usually do. This does not come naturally or easily, even though I know it is the right thing to do. Never before have I accepted his decisions without a fight. However, I am committed because I feel it is God's will.

It is very frightening to me that our daughter has reacted to this change in parenting by actually worsening her behavior and losing more weight. I am tempted to react as I have before by becoming fearful of having used wrong judgment, questioning the decision, and eventually changing the planned action in an attempt to improve the situation.

But I am different now and I respond differently. I am still afraid, but this is where I stop now. I don't give audience to thoughts of reacting, questioning, and attacking my husband, even though the immediate results appear wrong. For right now it is better to be consistent and possibly wrong than to keep changing decisions midstream. Hopefully our daughter will learn to trust that we cannot be manipulated or frightened into altering what we originally believed was best for her.

I know that for Shadrach, Meshach, and Abednego, the positive soon replaced the negative. For us it may be a longer time. How difficult it is to wait.

Lord, take away my fears and honor my obedience.

To Find Victory in You

A captive with no way out,
A slave to food and an even greater
Slave to defeatist thoughts and emotions…

My daughter is being held prisoner
By an eating disorder, Lord.
I want to storm the gates of her mind
Like a group of well-armed Marines
And blow the monster clear into eternity!
I don't like feeling helpless.
I hate even more for my child to feel
Helpless against this invisible foe.
She's a young woman with her whole
Life ahead of her. She's looked forward
To gaining her independence for so long.
Although she thought becoming an adult
Would give her freedom, she's finding no
Freedom in this adversity. Help her
To understand that adversity in life comes
To all of us in one form or another.
Please do not allow this fact to overwhelm
Her thoughts. Life is a series of one battle
After another. May she see this eating disorder
As one of the battles she must face, but not alone,
For we are with her all of the way, just as You are.
Help her to have the strength and faith to fight
One day at a time, depending upon You for her
Strength. In the overcoming of it, may she become
Stronger and more determined to win the
Next battle whenever or wherever it comes.
Give her hope and faith to find victory in You.

Communication

Fathers, do not exasperate your children; instead, bring them up in the training and instruction of the Lord. Ephesians 6:4

All relationships have conflict. For a partnership to be healthy, the conflict must be resolved. Communication is the tool by which we reveal ourselves, learn more about others, and resolve conflict. Expressing personal feelings and allowing others to do the same provides the fuel for discussion and the path for understanding each other.

Unfortunately, I only recently learned this. My problem has been that I expressed only one emotion: anger. I believed all other feelings were symptoms of weakness and should not be elaborated on. When my daughter or my wife would share their problems or concerns, I immediately embarked on a problem-solving mission to remove any of their negative emotions such as sorrow or fear. I saw these as having no value in a healthy person's life.

Needless to say, I was a conversation killer. Discussion with me never went much further than an initial attempt to express oneself before frustration set in. As a consequence, communication was limited to mis-interpretation and assumption, rather than a real understanding of what someone felt or thought. Before long my daughter became hindered in her ability to express herself, since attempts to do so had so often ended in defeat. She began to build a wall around herself, which safely closed her in and shut us out for many years. It was a long time before I realized that anger is not the only valid emotion. Jesus demonstrated many other emotions such as concern, helplessness, sorrow, and fear.

My newly found understanding is helping us all change. I am learning not to exasperate my daughter or wife, but rather to establish an honest and open dialogue. My daughter is lowering the walls and my wife feels connected to me again.

At Long Last, I Accept

...the battle is not yours, but God's. 2 Chronicles 20:15

It was a long night. I turned and repositioned myself for the hundredth time and finally fell into a restless sleep. Dreams spun in my head in rapid succession, each more troublesome than the previous one until at last I awakened to discover I was drenched in sweat. I was afraid of the possibility that my daughter might die. It was the first time I truly saw suicide as the horrific termination of a life before it could be lived in full. Now at 3:00 a.m., I wondered if many others like me were speaking to God. I found it a comforting thought that mine might be the lone voice God heard this early morning as I prayed:

> *Dear Lord, hear my cry for help for it will always be only You to whom I can turn. I have done so many things wrong in raising her. Even in these days I often say and do what I should not, but I am so afraid. I want to save her, but my greatest fear is that perhaps I can't. What lesson are You teaching me? Is it like Job's: that You are sovereign and can do as You will without question? Or am I learning what Abraham lived: accepting possible death for his son, Isaac, as a test of his faith in You? I have tried all I know to help my daughter, but one thing remains—one thing that I have never been able to do. I have never accepted the fact that I can't ensure how this will all end. But now, my ways are finished and my ideas are no more. I cannot change what is before me and I can only kneel at Your feet, God, and say the battle is not mine, but Yours. I will be still and accept what I cannot change. Whatever occurs, may You be glorified and Your will be done. Amen.*

This War Against Bulimia

Nothing is more comforting, Lord,
Than to know You stand by my
Daughter, my husband, and me
In this war against bulimia.
Even though the battle seems lonely
At times, I know You stand with us
And You will never forsake us…
And in the standing, You give strength
Beyond our greatest imagining.
Thank You, Lord, for Your unfailing
Strength to meet our helplessness.
Thank You, that in Your strength,
My daughter can find deliverance
From the disease that seeks
To rob her of life. Help her, Lord,
To recognize Your intervention
As the work of Your hand brings forth
Her deliverance, may she live to
Proclaim how Your hand upon her life
Has brought about her preservation.
May she always give You praise and glory
For her victory in the war!

Inspired by 2 Timothy 4:17-18

It's New Every Morning

We face what seems to be an insurmountable task: parenting daughters with eating disorders. Often it means encouraging them when we ourselves feel no hope. It may mean setting limits and disciplining when we don't know how. Sometimes it's seeking professional help when there is nowhere to look. It means loving them when love is not returned, and it means watching them hurt when we have no way to help.

Many times I've wept by my bed at night wondering how I would go on when all my desire seems to be lost. At those desperate times, I have recalled the verse spoken by David in the Bible:

Weeping may endure for a night, but joy cometh in the morning. Psalm 30:5 (KJV)

It is a promise of deliverance, despite the sorrow of the present. When I feel hopeless about a future of bondage to this disorder, I can only hope in God's mercies—that they are sufficient for coping with today and that God will give to me what I need to be able to face tomorrow. The book of Lamentations consists solely of passionate laments over the destruction of beloved Jerusalem. Yet, amidst his suffering, the author has a hope in the love and mercy of God:

I remember my affliction and my wandering, the bitterness and the gall. I well remember them, and my soul is downcast within me. Yet this I call to mind and therefore I have hope: Because of the LORD's great love we are not consumed, for his compassions never fail. They are new every morning; great is your faithfulness. I say to myself, "The LORD is my portion; therefore I will wait for him." Lamentations 3:19-24.

I don't know what the future will bring, but I do know that I can depend on the promises above—that God's mercies and love will not fail me. Whenever I feel like giving up at the end of a hard day, I must remind myself that my portion will be new tomorrow, and I will go on.

Our daughter's counselor has a small plaque in her office that I think is a sweet way of reminding me of this every time I'm in there. It reads:

Courage doesn't always roar. Sometimes courage is the quiet voice at the end of the day saying I will try again tomorrow.

Lord, Use Our Trials to Help Us Grow

Suppose a gardener purchases new gardening tools. Being industrious, he doesn't leave them hanging in the work shed, but takes them into the garden to use. He carefully tills the soil with his new tools, preparing the spot to place his living plant.

This story to me is an analogy of the counseling process. We are the gardeners and the tools are the techniques we acquire through counseling. If the circumstances and trials of life can be thought of as the soil, then our tools "dig" into the dirt, uncovering areas below the surface that need new life planted. The fragile living plant is our soul, vulnerably placed and created to grow.

However, tools have their limitations. It's not just them, but the nutrients in the soil, along with the rain and the sun that create the growth in the plant. Tools help, but only God's workmanship creates new life. So it is for us. God alone masterfully uses the trials and circumstances, the soil in which our soul lives, to nurture our character. And God alone abundantly pours upon us the cleansing rain of His forgiveness and bathes us in the warm sun of His love.

Just as the plants flourish under nature's provision, we flourish through God's faithful and endless care. We deepen our roots, grow to new heights, and finally bloom.

Consider it pure joy, my brothers, whenever you face trials of many kinds, because you know that the testing of your faith develops perseverance. Perseverance must finish its work so that you may be mature and complete, not lacking anything.
James 1:2-4

There's a Kitten Up a Tree

There's a kitten up a tree,
I hear its tiny cry.
It climbed there on its own,
And now it's mewing helplessly.
In looking back
The way it came,
The view is different, changed,
Dangerous, even scary.
Where are the places
It put its tiny paws
In order to reach the height
To which it now clings?
I don't know, the kitten whines.
All I know is I'm scared
And I can't come down by myself.
The mewing continues.
Doesn't anyone else hear what I hear?
This kitten is my child, Lord.
I'd prefer to be the Mama Cat
And climb out on the limb
To rescue my kitten,
But the limb won't support both of us.
We'd only fall to harm.
I need You, Lord—
Quickly, if You will.
I trust You, Lord,
To safely catch my child
Before she hits the ground below.

God's Reminders

Be still and know that I am God. Psalm 46:10

Have you ever stood beneath trees reaching hundreds of feet above your own height and contemplated the insignificance of your own stature? Have you considered their majesty punctuated by the final rays of the day's sun illuminating the branches? Have you watched a hawk float above, much higher than you could ever reach, wings spread in absolute defiance of gravity? Have you considered the strength of lightning, decisively claiming its target? Or the authority of the thunder proclaiming it shall be heard?

So complex in their creation and yet so simple to observe—the green of the trees in stately pose, the call of a single hawk against a cloudless sky, the darkness of a night penetrated by a flash of light and roar of thunder. There is a peace in the simplicity of it all, for in its existence, it remains so certain and so unmindful of time.

When our days are wrought with failure or our own weakness defeats us, it is comforting to seek refuge in the serenity of nature. Placing our daily tasks and concerns against the grandeur of God's workmanship makes it easier to gain a proper perspective of our own lives. Here, our frailty is vulnerable to the power and sovereignty of God and we can only kneel in reverence and humility, quieting our troubled selves before Him.

Even When You Do Not Know It

Tucson is a desert town surrounded on all sides by mountains. During the winter months when cold rain washes the city, clouds often lay low, hiding the mountain from view. After a few days, the storm passes through the valley, taking with it the clouds and rain, leaving in return a brilliant, clear blue sky and definite mountains. Resumed visibility often means the likelihood of an exhilarating discovery that God has decorated the mountaintops with a dusting of pure white snow that crowns this sleepy western town with majesty.

Occasionally, I feel like my vision is shrouded in clouds. Living with a daughter recovering from anorexia is often like living in that valley during a rainstorm. My visibility is impaired to anything beyond today and its immediate problems. I can't see any eternal benefits, make any sense out of what's happening, or see the direction of where I am going. But then there are these glorious periods when life makes sense and I can even see some benefit from all the pain, just as the clouds clear to reveal the beautiful result of the storm. At those times, I feel as if I've discovered a treasure of how God is completing His good and perfect will. I wish my vision was never impaired, but since it is not that way, in faith I must believe Paul's words in Romans:

> *Who hopes for what he already has? But if we hope for what we do not yet have, we wait for it patiently. In the same way, the Spirit helps us in our weakness. We do not know what we ought to pray for, but the Spirit himself intercedes for us with groans that words cannot express. And he who searches our hearts knows the mind of the Spirit, because the Spirit intercedes for the saints in accordance with God's will. And we know that in all things God works for the good of those who love him, who have been called according to his purpose.* Romans 8:24-28

Family Friendships

If you have any encouragement from being united with Christ,
if any comfort from his love, if any fellowship with the Spirit, if
any tenderness and compassion, then make my joy complete
by being like-minded, having the same love, being one in spirit
and purpose. Do nothing out of selfish ambition or vain con-
ceit, but in humility consider others better than yourselves.
Each of you should look not only to your own interests, but
also to the interests of others. Philippians 2:1-4

Families of eating-disordered individuals often experience dysfunction. The usual imperfections of relationships present in most families can be greatly magnified by the presence of an eating disorder. The strain of an unresolved problem pulls and stretches the threads of relationships apart, clearly exposing all the holes and flaws. Relationships with our parents are studied, problems with our spouse are exposed, and our own parenting habits are scrutinized. It is hurtful to lay all the ugliness and sin, all the weaknesses and selfishness out in the open and realize the pain it has caused. To leave it there without beginning a process of repairing and rebuilding a healthy family would be relationally disastrous and personally devastating.

As this verse states, laying the foundation for the future is best constructed upon a solid ground of shared belief. How much easier it is to mend family relationships when members have the same belief. But what should be done with relatives who do not? God can still provide us with tenderness and compassion to reach out to them with unselfish motives, acting on what we believe to be for their best.

My personal challenge has been the unhealthy habits that have persisted from my mother to me and from me to my daughter. Because most eating-disordered individuals are girls and women, the relationship between mothers and daughters are quick targets for trouble. I felt it was important to break these longstanding negative patterns and build healthy ones.

This very day I completed a letter to my mom expressing my love. It is true that there are some unexpressed hurts and some unresolved problems. However, we have been able to mend greatly despite the age of my mom and her inability to understand this new era of counseling. There are still some issues better left untouched for now. Maybe those will be resolved later.

I encourage you to pause today and consider someone within your family to whom you can extend an invitation to build a healthier and more loving friendship. God will give you the words to say, if you will risk the love.

I Need to Grow Through This

Dear God,
In the midst of all my troubles,
I suddenly realize that I am afraid:
Afraid of finding out I've been wrong
In the way I've behaved,
The way I've loved my daughter.
I want to dance around the issues
And talk about her behavior now
And the results of it.

I now ask myself where I'm to blame,
But this is the wrong question.
I need to grow through this,
Not shrivel and shrink.
I need to be able to accept responsibility
For my own actions,
But not in a condemning way.

I need to feel that as a family,
We're an integral part of one another.
We're living together, loving together,
So we need to grow together—
Emotionally and spiritually.
When we somehow manage
To stunt that growth in one another,
We've made a mistake.
But mistakes can be undone,
Especially once they're recognized,
And owned-up to.

All of us make mistakes.
No one is perfect, Lord, except You.

Strengthen us in Your love enough
For us to feel we can outgrow
The places, the behaviors, the attitudes
In our lives that do not reflect Your love.

Already Accepted

I was having a conversation with my daughter one day about her fear of never being able to please God. She admits that not caring for her body properly because of her anorexia is disobedience to God's commands and results in His displeasure. But an anorexic's constant fear is that an ideal place is unattainable because eating anything more than the restricted amount will result in out-of-control eating. In essence, she views her choice as between anorexia or obesity. If she must choose one over the other, she will choose the former. This thinking is a significant hindrance to her complete recovery and to freedom in eating.

Because I have never had an eating disorder, it is very difficult for me to understand this line of thinking. We have a communication gap whenever she tries to express her thoughts. But on this particular day, the realization struck me that she was struggling with a spiritual issue that might possibly be one of works versus grace. Often a component of anorexia is perfectionism, and perfectionism is related to a works-oriented faith. It goes something like this: If one can always be good, then God will put on His stamp of approval and acceptance on us and love will be achieved. Always being good, of course, means one must never diverge from the path of absolute self-control because the cost of doing so is tremendous—God's rejection.

My daughter doesn't understand that God's commitment to us is without condition because He already knows the outcome of all of our actions and He has extended His grace with this foreknowledge. We are important because God wants us as His own and we are secure because of His performance on our behalf, not because of our performance on His behalf. Our good works are an outgrowth of our salvation and our assurance that we already are accepted, never the reverse. Paul states this clearly in his letter to the church at Ephesus.

For it is by grace you have been saved, through faith—and this not from yourselves, it is the gift of God—not by works, so that no one can boast. For we are God's workmanship, created in Christ Jesus to do good works, which God prepared in advance for us to do. Ephesians 2:8-10

I asked my daughter this question, "When you are standing at the gate to heaven someday and God asks you why you should be here, would you say it's because of what you have done or would you say it's because of what Jesus has done?"

Help During the Battle

The book of Exodus relates the journey of the Israelites from captivity in Egypt to the promised land of Canaan. Their leader Moses, was authorized by God to lead them into battle against the opposing armies. One such battle is described in Exodus 17:10-13.

So Joshua fought the Amalekites as Moses had ordered, and Moses, Aaron and Hur went to the top of the hill. As long as Moses held up his hands, the Israelites were winning, but whenever he lowered his hands, the Amalekites were winning. When Moses' hands grew tired, they took a stone and put it under him and he sat on it. Aaron and Hur held his hands up—one on one side, one on the other—so that his hands remained steady till sunset. So Joshua overcame the Amalekite army with the sword.

How good is the help of a friend. There are two women who have been by my side through the past six years. They have been my mentors, my confidantes, and my friends. I've grown tired of fighting the battle and I've relied on their alliances to empower me. When I've had victories, they've been there to rejoice and praise God for answered prayer. Many other people through these difficult years have been blessings to my husband and to me, but I am especially thankful for these two faithful saints God placed in my life.

A friend loves at all times, and a brother is born for adversity. Proverbs 17:17

Relationship With My Wife

Husbands, love your wives, just as Christ loved the church and gave himself up for her. Ephesians 5:25

By the grace of God, my wife and I have been married for 26 years. I say by the grace of God because we had to depend on His forgiveness and His direction in order to survive. For more than half of those years we subordinated our relationship to everything else in our lives. Our time spent just as a couple never took priority over duties at home and work, and especially over the children. We were enemies more days than we were friends, and we used our differences as weapons to threaten each other or defend ourselves. She seemed always upset about something, so I learned to tune her out and not respond to her constant concerns. Another fault was that I saw my wife as having more spiritual tendencies than I have, so I left it to her to be the "spiritual one." She was the one who had to initiate communal prayer or share biblical insight.

The result was a subtle resentment in our relationship. She never felt I listened to her and I always thought she was too emotional. We did not experience the joy that can come when two people use their differences to their advantage rather than to their detriment. It wasn't until I learned that most women and men usually do not feel, think, or act the same that I began to listen to and value what my wife had to say. By assigning worth to her opinions, I gave her merit as an individual. She was more able to recognize when her emotions were doing her thinking. Our marriage began to bloom.

We are now learning to recognize the value of a team approach and give priority to quality time together as a couple. I thank God for helping me see my shortcomings. Sometimes the greatest gains come through the pain of having to face ourselves because our daughter has an eating disorder.

He Makes the Crooked Paths Straight

Consider the work of God; for who can make that straight, which he has made crooked? In the day of prosperity be joyful, but in the day of adversity consider: God also hath set the one over against the other. Ecclesiastes 7:13-14 (KJV)

The "straight" in life is when things are fitting together nicely and the "crooked" is when the puzzle pieces appear jumbled, including the blunders and messes we create for ourselves. I have spent a lot of time worrying about my daughter's problems. I fear her eating disorder will ruin God's plan for her life. When I fear that her crooked path will never be made straight, I remember the story of Joseph, a man whose difficulties became steppingstones to God's purposes.

In Genesis 37:5-11, Joseph dreams two different dreams, the content being that Joseph is depicted as ruling over his brothers. With some arrogance and with motives less than noble, he tells his brothers about the dreams, infuriating them to the point of seeking revenge by selling him into captivity. The "crooked" in Joseph's life originates first by his own poor choice, and secondly, by the brothers' evil schemes. Joseph is sold into slavery and ends up in Egypt. Despite this, God intervenes. Joseph rises to power and is the one who supplies grain to his own people, the Israelites, during a severe famine. As Joseph tells his remorseful brothers, *"You intended to harm me, but God intended it for good to accomplish what is now being done, the saving of many lives."* Genesis 50:20

If God is indeed sovereign and in control of all things, then I need to let go of my responsibility for my daughter's future and let her experience the consequences of her "crooked" choices. Indeed! I can trust God to work all according to His good and perfect plan. He will make the crooked paths straight.

The Need for the Invisible Line

Lord, there's nothing worse for us as parents
Than feeling helpless when our child is hurting.
As her mother, help me to feel less guilt
And pity—for these feelings only lead
To disappointment, frustration, and anger—
None of which add anything positive
To the situation. Help me outgrow
My mother's *fix-it* syndrome while
Remaining confident that there is victory
Ahead for our child. Help me to discern
Where I can help and where I would hinder
Should I become too involved.
We are beginning to see the need for the
Invisible line You've drawn, Lord. Maybe
We have finally reached it. Perhaps this is
The place here and now where You
Are saying, ***It's time to stop struggling
And worrying. It's time to allow Me to work
While teaching your child to depend upon Me.***
I begin to realize, Lord, that we, as parents,
Can become so caught up in feeling
Responsible and trying to help that we become
More a part of the problem and less and less
A part of the solution. Help us to help our child
Without becoming the crutch which enables.
I see now that none of us can find any long-term
Solution without our daughter developing her own
System of accountability. Give her the desire and
Confidence she needs to overcome this
Eating disorder, Lord. Help her overcome the

Deep-seated fears that seem to rule her life
Right now. Give each of us Your grace and
Mercy in dealing with the entire situation.
Help us gain our strength, wisdom, and peace
From You that we may teach our child
To do the same.

"Whistle While You Work"

Snow White's seven little dwarfs had the right idea for not being cantankerous. Just "whistle while you work," they chimed together as they marched off to the mines!

This simple advice is actually quite wise. Several years ago, I went through a period when I woke up every morning in a grumpy mood. It was at the height of my daughter's anorexia and I actually dreaded each day. I saw my life as "a glass half empty" rather than "half full." I had a lot of headaches in those days, along with other physical problems such as back and neck aches. I even had examinations to determine if the causes were more significant than muscle strain. I always considered pessimism the quality of being realistic for I never saw circumstances through rose-tinted glasses.

Because I often experienced depression, I was compelled to examine my perspective on life or else remain in anguish. I knew I needed to change my pessimistic outlook.

One change I made was to begin each day with a prayer of thanks. It was difficult some mornings to think even of one thing to say, but I forced myself to be creative. I continued this practice throughout the day. Whenever something arose that triggered my negative attitude, I would think of some way to give thanks for it.

Another practice I began was to sing whenever I felt the commencement of a headache. Astoundingly enough, the headaches would often subside.

I have since come to believe that looking at life from a negative viewpoint is really a defense mechanism to prevent ever being caught out of control. If I can anticipate everything that could go wrong and prepare accordingly, I would not be surprised by situations I could not handle. In addition, I would be protected from disappointment because I had already expected the worse!

God has replaced my approach to life with one that is much healthier. He revealed to me that His sovereign control and His grace is sufficient for all my circumstances. I do not need protection from difficulties, for each difficulty offers an opportunity for growth.

I think Solomon might agree with the dwarfs' philosophy because he says in Proverbs:

A cheerful heart is good medicine, but a crushed spirit dries up the bones. (17:22)

A happy heart makes the face cheerful, but heartache crushes the spirit. (15:13)

Rest the Stress

Ask anyone you know to describe what causes stress and I guarantee they can! Whether it be typed as excessive demands, chronic pain, trauma, change, threats or losses, they all result in the body's physical, mental, emotional, and chemical reaction to disruption. Stress is the body's preparation for handling the unfamiliar or the frightening. In normal circumstances, we have an arousal of some sort that causes the body's hormonal systems to activate for a period of time. This is followed by an interval of rest and recuperation. If the activation is prolonged or the rest is nonexistent, a cycle develops of chronic stress. This is what happens in a family dealing with an eating disorder.

I spend so much time just pedaling harder and faster, cycling like a mad woman through the streets of life. I don't take time to pause and evaluate until I'm burned out and forced to stop. During this cessation, I block out external stimuli as much as possible to focus on God. I slow down all my daily functions and include only those necessary for existence. In essence, I surrender my time to listen for God's message.

The principle of the Sabbath, as mandated by God in the Ten Commandments, provides for a day of absolute rest in order to be refreshed and renewed. Resting really means to trust because when one isn't working, it is necessary to depend on God to work. If I follow this as a preventative, not as a cure, I would most likely not experience burnout so often.

Forgive me, Lord, for not listening to Your words:

In repentance and rest is your salvation, in quietness and trust is your strength. Isaiah 30:15

Redefine the Negative

My daughter is a senior this year in a relatively tough, inner city district. Because it is her first year in a new school, she doesn't have many acquaintances or extracurricular activities. She frequently has bad days, but is trying to make the best of this year and enjoy the advantages of a different school with more diversity and observable experiences. One day while she was talking with me about school the phone rang. It was a friend of mine asking how my daughter liked school. My daughter could tell what course the conversation took and she remained in the room to listen. For questions like these I am normally so explicit I would say, "She likes it but has a difficult time," even proceeding to list the difficulties. But today I had an idea. Instead I said, "She is doing just fine!" When I hung up the phone, my daughter was noticeably pleased and remarked how appreciative she was for my answer. I was glad I had reinforced the positive rather than the negative.

To redefine a negative situation in a positive way is one of the newest concepts I am trying to master. It is my normal temperament to dwell on the negative, especially my daughter's negative characteristics because so many are associated with anorexia. In fact, every failure precipitates in my mind, "Here we go again, we are going down!" But now, instead of expecting her to fail, I want to invite her to be a winner! I am now trying to follow what the Bible has always proclaimed.

Do not let any unwholesome talk come out of your mouths, but only what is helpful for building others up according to their needs, that it may benefit those who listen. Ephesians 4:29

Life on Our Terms

Five of them were foolish and five were wise. Matthew 25:2

A kind man describes the sorrow he feels because his homosexual brother is dying of AIDS. He is angry with God when he hears that homosexuality is a sin that is condemned in the Bible.

A recovering alcoholic is searching for a god who makes her feel good about herself. She does not want to hear that God judges sin and says there are consequences to her behavior.

An anorexic daughter starves herself as a defense against the pain she has encountered. She is angry with God for allowing hurt to wound her youth.

In Matthew 25:1-13 some foolish guests want to enter the kingdom of heaven without oil in their lamps. When they finally realize it is a necessary requirement, the door is already closed.

There is a common theme in each of the above situations. The man, the alcoholic, the daughter, and the guests all believe God should be a reflection of their beliefs; instead, our beliefs should reflect God's nature. They want life on their terms and they want a feel-good God who will create it for them. When God allows suffering or when God acts as judge, He does not fit into their picture of an accepting and loving Supreme Being. As a result, God is relegated to a subordinate role. Ironically, they are waging a losing battle against a sovereign God.

God's wisdom reconciles these two attributes: justice and love. However, we cannot often comprehend how they can coexist in someone who always works in our best interests. For this reason it is best that we accept life as God plans it and stop trying to change it to fit our logic. In actuality we deserve little, and it is only because of God's love that we have anything good. Simple arrogance would cause us to think otherwise.

Triangles

Through counseling I have learned about a concept called triangulation. In a good relationship, intimacy is only possible between two people when there is both safety and pleasure. When stress occurs, the goodwill between the couple can be jeopardized and a third party is then brought in to take the pressure off. This can be a counselor, someone who is impartial and objective enough to give a perspective the other two cannot see. However, the third party may not be an objective person; instead, it may be someone who creates more difficulties.

For example, a teen with an eating disorder does not get along well with a father who is detached from both her and her mother, especially mom who continually pleads with dad to engage. If he does engage, it is never in the manner the mother or daughter desires. As a result, mother and daughter form an alliance against the father. This manifests itself in a variety of ways. When the daughter has a problem with the father, she tells the mother who then informs the father of what he is doing wrong with his daughter. Or, the daughter wants to do something so she goes to the mother to get approval. The mother either fails to consult with the father or if she does, allies with the daughter anyway. A triangle is formed, but the points are not at even distances. The father stands alienated from the other two and is depicted as a villain.

Triangulation is strangulation to relationships. There is no winner. The mother remains enmeshed, rescuing the daughter from her father. The daughter, who is physically unhealthy, stays in control forcing all to cater to her problem. She does not take personal responsibility to resolve conflict. The father remains stuck. He receives little love and respect from wife or daughter and lacks the ability to express his own feelings. Destroying this triangle requires much work over a long period of time, and there is no certainty that in doing so the relationships will be restored. However, if the attempt is never made, the health of the relationship will be in even greater danger.

There is another triangle that can be formed in a family relationship that is stable and healthy. It involves Jesus Christ. The husband and the wife are at two different points in the triangle. The Lord is at the third point above them. They can go to Him together or separately and He will not make alliances with one over the other because He treats them both equally. He will never portray one as the villain and the other as the hero. In fact, He will hold each accountable for his/her own part. He always has both of their best interests at heart. With God as our ally, we are strong.

If God is for us, who can be against us? Romans 8:31

An alliance among the husband, the wife, and Jesus Christ forms a triangle of safety that strengthens intimacy and provides a stable and consistent family environment for the children.

An Unexpected Gift

My palms are sweaty and my back aches. My tension feels like a steel rod running along the length of my spine, stretching my muscles and nerves. The receptionist announces that the doctor is ready to see us. Carrying myself with authority, I follow my husband, making certain that my confidence is evident.

"We came to see you today because I recommended to my wife that she ask about the possibility of taking anti-depressants," my husband stated.

"I don't really want to take them," I quickly responded, "but I agreed to consider this option."

"What are your reasons for and against the medication?" the doctor inquired.

"They could be a help when I get very depressed. But even when I'm depressed I'm still able to function. Therefore, I don't want to put up with the inconvenience of monitoring them and adjusting to them," I replied. In reality I was thinking: I can handle my *emotions* on my own and I don't need any crutch.

After further discussion, the doctor handed me a prescription. "Consider our conversation during the upcoming days," he said, "then make your own decision as to whether or not to take the medication."

My mind wandered to a time two years before when it was first recommended that my daughter take Prozac. I was torn between knowing she needed something to relieve her unhappiness, and yet feeling that only psychiatric patients take medication. I finally acknowledged my daughter's need because her problem was so serious; but as for me, I had confidence I could control the severity of my depression.

"I am afraid that we are entering into a period when my wife's emotions will be taxed." My husband's concern was evident. The deadline for our daughter to meet the necessary weight requirement for attending Arizona State University next fall is just two months away. Early indications are that she will not meet the deadline, and my wife has already had some violent emotional attacks as a result."

"I have fought anti-depressants for years because I really want to prove that God's grace is sufficient for all my troubles—not some artificial substance." I said this, clearly knowing that I was confused.

"Drugs aren't going to be a substitute for a relationship with God," the doctor explained. "They merely stop you from fighting an uphill battle against what might be a chemical imbalance in your brain. It is really not much different from taking antibiotics for an infection. You do take those, don't you?" He was not sarcastic, but interested.

"Of course I do. Perhaps it is a contradiction to take the one and not the other. It just seems like such a sign of weakness to be on psychotropic medication. I don't want to admit that I can't do it on my own." I surprised myself with my honesty.

"Have you considered that God already knows about your weaknesses and your strengths? He is omniscient and knows everything about you. In Psalms it says, 'before a word is on my tongue You know it completely, O LORD.' He knows that we are all fragile for the psalmist also says that 'He knows how we are formed, He remembers that we are dust.' " Tears welled up in my eyes when I heard my husband's words.

He continued, "If God is omniscient, then He knows the future. Maybe this is His plan to protect you from your volatile emotions and enable you to get through future difficulties in a manner that is glorifying to Him."

I know deep in my heart that we had set a course of action we intended to keep in order to set limits for our daughter, and I would not turn from it. I wanted more than anything else to be able to support and work with my husband and to let our daughter grow in independence. I couldn't fool myself that it would be an easy road ahead. I realized I needed to be in the best state of mind to go on this journey and that might mean traveling with some medication.

I had made my decision. "I will try them beginning next week. Maybe it's true that they could be an unexpected gift from God."

My Emotions and His Justice

"I feel like I am being held under water and your hand is the one that's pushing me down. All the while you tell me that I shouldn't feel like I'm drowning." These are the very words I said to my husband last month. It is a perfect picture of my feelings whenever we have an argument that arouses intensity within me.

The pattern is always the same. First, our daughter manifests her anorexic behaviors to the point that I am facing a worrisome situation. Feeling distraught, I tell my husband that something has to be done and he rationally replies that we can do nothing. I struggle against his stoicism until our debate reaches a climax and words become piercing and hateful. I am an emotional wreck, watching him calmly and solidly stand his ground. I react as an active volcano spewing venomous fire over him, so violent in my eruption that even I am alarmed by the intensity.

I perceive my husband to be a very insensitive person, one who won't sympathize with my fears or cater to my emotions. In fact, his apparent insensitivity angers me so much that I shut off every opportunity for him to reason with me or communicate the logic behind his opposing decision. In the end, our arguments leave us both feeling fatally wounded. Our marriage is being ripped apart by the effects of this eating disorder, and I don't know how to stop it.

I conveyed this to a confidante who fortunately was very honest with me. She pointed out that I focus so much on the hurt caused by my husband's insensitivity that I miss the truth behind his message. The fact that I am in pain negates everything else.

I considered her statement and discovered it to be true. My husband had been right and I had been wrong. However, I don't like to be told to do something I don't completely agree with, so I use the excuse of not being treated sensitively. By doing this I can transfer the blame and avoid the humility of admitting I am wrong.

Oh God, when I am so preoccupied with myself that I don't hear Your truth, dispense Your justice. Help me see past my emotions and stubbornness to what is right and true and just. Help me learn that obeying You and Your righteous word is more important than how I feel.

The LORD…is righteous;
He does no wrong.
Morning by morning he dispenses his justice,
And every new day he does not fail,
Yet the unrighteous know no shame. Zephaniah 3:5

Life's Race

At the 200-meter mark, my daughter had a twenty-yard lead and was pulling away from the nearest competitor. She crossed the finish line, surrounded by her teammates. She was the new 1600-meter champion, setting a league record in the process. This proud father stood in the stands, cheering loudly with a wide, proud grin across his face.

Six months later, that same daughter was in another race…a race for her life. We had to move quickly to get her help. She had already lost 25 pounds since her record-setting run, and now inpatient treatment was her new challenge.

Today, she is progressing well and has accepted the fact that she will never be in competitive athletics again. Today's race is different. It is for life and the hope of recovery. In this race there is no stopwatch or record to be broken. It is a slow process with many hurdles. Persistent effort is necessary if recovery is to become a reality.

God's word speaks of this life race in Philippians 3:14.

I press on toward the goal for the prize of the upward call in Christ Jesus. (NASB)

I am learning to encourage inner personal progress instead of athletic accomplishment in my loved ones, no matter how far away from the "mark" they be, just as Christ encourages me!

Sin Is Sin...Forgiveness a Must

It is midmorning, yet shadows drape the rooms of my house with a dreary darkness. Although the constant drizzle of rain outside cannot get in the house, I still feel it. Cold and damp penetrate my soul. I spent last evening sorting through photo albums and old pictures, including ones of my daughter taken before her eating disorder. They had proven to be a shocking contrast to her current hollow cheeks and emaciated frame.

I am reminded of how devastating disobedience can be, and how sin is absolutely deplorable to a holy God. I often wonder if my daughter's eating disorder is a choice or if the compulsive aspect removes it from free will. I may never know the answer to that, but I do know that her eating disorder causes her to miss out on God's blessings. It cannot be something that God would desire for her life, and that thought deeply saddens me.

My daily sins are less evident, but as equally destructive as an eating disorder. They drag me down and tie weights to my ankles when I run the race of life. According to the book of Romans, I am no better than my daughter.

For all have sinned and fall short of the glory of God, and are justified freely by his grace through the redemption that came by Christ Jesus. Romans 3:23-24

Jesus bore an unimaginable burden when He voluntarily hung on the cross and bore the full weight of the sin of the world. When I read a news article about a hideous crime, I am filled with disgust at man's depravity. When these sins are combined with every other sin throughout the history of the world, it's overwhelming to realize that Jesus chose to take the cup. *"My Father, if it is possible, let this cup pass from Me; yet not as I will, but as You will."* Matthew 26:39 (NASB)

81

When we see clearly all the pain and the sorrow disobedience causes us and those we love, our proper response is to seek the Savior who can heal those wounds and ask for His forgiveness.

As this day of rain draws to an end and the first rays of a sunset venture forth through the clouds, I feel a great peace in welcoming its light. I think the dreariness of the day is much like sin, and the sunlight is like God's forgiveness that brings joy and restoration.

> *For as high as the heavens are above the earth, so great is his love for those who fear him; as far as the east is from the west, so far has he removed our transgressions from us. As a father has compassion on his children, so the LORD has compassion on those who fear him.* Psalm 103:11-13

Words Which Never Should Have Been Spoken

Lord, I've just realized something—
Not only have I harbored anger in my own life,
I've helped to create it in the life of my child.
I made the mistake of using my child as a
Friend—sharing personal hurts I had no right
To dump upon a child. Now there is anger,
Bitterness, and resentment where I would
Have lovingly placed acceptance, encouragement,
And self-worth. Oh, the ache of never being
Able to retract words that never should have
Been spoken. Anger is like cancer, only worse.
It not only eats at the heart which holds
And nurtures it, it also spreads to innocents
And destroys them as well.

God, I'm so sorry.
Forgive me for using my child's ears to spill
Out my own bitterness and anger. Help my
Child to forgive me some day. Undo the
Harm I've caused in whatever way You choose
To work in our lives. Please work to prevent
My lips from doing more harm to
Those I love so much.

Blessed Are the Humble

Blessed are the meek, for they will inherit the earth. Matthew 5:5

Jesus promises blessing to the person whose disposition before God is one of humility: consciousness of one's own shortcomings. The proud will not inherit treasures in eternity, but rather the meek will receive the riches of which the proud would boast.

Jesus often says to learn from Him through the instruction of the Holy Spirit and to follow Him. This instruction implies the necessity of being taught and assumes the attitude of humility.

In the years that an individual has an eating disorder, the time spent in counseling offices is colossal; therefore, it presents an enormous opportunity for humility and learning. It is very difficult for us as parents to swallow our pride when being told that we are unhealthy individuals and have a dysfunctional marriage and family. It is equally difficult to see our daughter listening to advice from other adults instead of from us, and to sit in a room during a "truth in love" session disclosing our family problems in front of a dozen people.

However, if we are not willing to humble ourselves and learn from others, we cannot learn from Jesus. We need to submit ourselves to God and His instruction, embracing not part but all that is being said. For *"God opposes the proud but gives grace to the humble."* James 4:6

Intercessory Prayer

I ask on their behalf... John 17:9 (NASB)

When my husband and I were in college, we had a minister friend who directed the college group at church. One time we were perplexed about a problem and my husband sought out this friend for advice. After the meeting, it was reported to me with some disgust that the only help the minister offered was to pray for us. We were not Christians then, so we both laughed at the superficial and obviously naïve approach to resolving the problem! Now we know better.

Intercessory prayer: to make requests on behalf of another. Jesus did this often. One of the most tender and intimate passages in the Bible is John 17 which records Jesus' final words to His disciples before His arrest and crucifixion. Jesus prays to His Father on behalf of His beloved followers. He intimately expresses His desire for them to be strengthened for impending tribulation and equipped for the hard work before them.

It means so much to me now when friends say they will pray for me. Every week for ten years, two friends and I have gathered to pray for each other. I can almost picture the sweet incense rising to heaven! My family is constantly being lifted up and asked to be placed directly into the center of God's will, week after week after week.

Praying for my daughter to overcome anorexia is something I don't use as a last resort, nor is it a superficial or naïve approach to her problems. Persistent, meaningful intercessory prayer for someone we love, coming from the depths of our believing hearts, will reach the attentive ear of God.

Mama, Pray for Me

She's my child and Yours, Lord.
I acknowledge she's Yours first
And only on loan to me.

I love her so much, Lord,
So You're used to hearing
Her name in my prayers.

Each time life gets hard
And she doesn't know
If she can deal with the stress,
Her words nearly break my heart
And put me on my knees.

I'm here again, Lord.
On behalf of the child
We share and love together.

You heard her plea last night,
Nevertheless, I bring her
To Your throne of grace
And leave her there with You
As I act upon her request,
Mama, pray for me.

The Balance—Time for Yourself

The miracle of Jesus feeding the 5,000 people from five loaves of bread and two fish has been told repeatedly. The events following this miracle are also quite meaningful. The people were stunned with amazement at what happened. They began to shout, demanding that Jesus become their King (John 6:15). They were so insistent and so likely to get out of control that Jesus ordered His disciples to get into the boat and go on ahead of him to the other side, while he dismissed the crowd. Jesus knew when to stop His work and seek time alone.

> *After he had dismissed them, he went up on a mountainside by himself to pray. When evening came, he was there alone, but the boat was already a considerable distance from land.*
> Matthew 14:23

Jesus was likely giving thanks for the miracle, and praying for these difficult people who wanted a political, not spiritual, answer to their life problems. How would He restrain their political ambitions for Him and how would the disciples be trained for the work ahead? This time away from His disciples, ministry, and the demands of everyday life provided Jesus the opportunity to enjoy indescribable communion with His Father. He was refreshed and ready to perform His next miracle by walking across the water to rejoin His friends in the boat.

We also need to learn when to stop our work and seek time alone. We get so involved in caring for our family's needs, especially during troubled times, that we often won't allow ourselves to indulge in relaxation or hobbies. We miss the opportunity to enjoy outside interests and to take our minds off the eating disorder. As a mother who is accustomed to nurturing, I find this especially hard for two reasons. The first is that my daughter has isolated herself from most of her friends, causing her to be alone much of the day and night. It breaks my heart to leave and pursue my own interests. Secondly, I am likely to feel guilty if I spend energy and money on my own activities. However, I have to remind myself of the need for balance in all things. I need to also remember that in healthy relationships there must be a balance between unity and individuality. When both are present, family members are free to be separate and yet choose to be bonded in friendship. I believe if we follow Jesus' example, we will better persevere through our trials.

His Yoke Is Easy and His Burden Is Light

In Jesus' day, a man would buy an ox and take it to a carpenter who measured its shoulders and made a yoke to fit. Some poor oxen must have suffered horribly under badly fitting yokes. However, a good carpenter would make sure the yoke was perfectly adjusted to the build of the ox. The oxen were yoked together so they would not have to pull the load alone. In this way, the team could pull the load easily with little pain. Jesus was probably remembering His days as a carpenter when He spoke the following.

> *Come to me, all you who are weary and burdened, and I will give you rest. Take my yoke upon you and learn from me, for I am gentle and humble in heart, and you will find rest for your souls. For my yoke is easy and my burden is light.*
> Matthew 11:28-30

Jesus' promise tells us that we are made for God, so we can be yoked together with Him. Jesus measures and custom fits His yoke for each of us so that we are able to pull our load in life and be perfectly adjusted to the purpose for which we are created.

When we feel overwhelmed, let's take time to look at our burden. Are we causing friction by rebelling against the yoke He has placed on us? Are we trying to pull the load alone? Is it a yoke we have made for ourselves by taking on what we should not?

Let us first come to Him and seek His yoke and rest. Let Him adjust our yoke to fit us so that He can work through the burden we bear and cause us to see meaning and future blessing from it.

We Are Rooted and Established in Love

But God demonstrates his ownlove for us in this: While we were still sinners, Christ died for us. Romans 5:8

When I think about this simple yet profound statement, I remember a time, a number of years ago, when God reached out to me. It was not because I had done anything special to make Him want to do that. I was so pathetic and undeserving that I certainly could not offer Him anything He needed. I was far from His holiness, yet He loved me enough to span the chasm between my sinfulness and His righteousness. Christ reached across the chasm and touched me.

I learned about God from that experience. I cannot make God love me any more or less by doing better or trying harder. I never have been, nor ever will be perfect. God sees me as righteous only because He looks at me through the veil of Jesus' blood. How wonderful to know that I am loved eternally. To know this love takes away my fears and gives me peace.

I pray that you, being rooted and established in love, may have power, together with all the saints, to grasp how wide and long and high and deep is the love of Christ, and to know this love that surpasses knowledge—that you may be filled to the measure of all the fullness of God. Ephesians 3:17-19

Spiritual Warfare

I have always felt that any personal or relational problem has a spiritual component. We are not just flesh and blood, but also, spirit. It is the spiritual part of man that has inspired many to greatness. It is also in the union of our spirit with God's that we find peace and fulfillment.

In dealing with life-threatening eating disorders, I believe it wise to also consider the existence of spiritual warfare—the possibility of a problem being empowered by evil spiritual forces. My experience with and knowledge of this is very limited, but there are times I feel I am opposing a force behind this eating disorder that is not merely human. The oppression on my daughter and on our family seems as if it is generated from a powerful being in the unseen world. I can almost visualize demons dancing around in our house, tormenting us and scheming to rob us of our joy and peace.

In the following passage, Paul emphasizes that all of us need to arm ourselves against these destructive hidden powers. I am to arm myself daily, stand my ground firmly, and look to God for the victory. My opponent may be Satan himself, but my advocate is Almighty God and He is the Victorious One.

Finally, be strong in the Lord, and in his mighty power. Put on the full armor of God so that you can take your stand against the devil's schemes. For our struggle is not against flesh and blood, but against the rulers, against the authorities, against the powers of this dark world and against the spiritual forces of evil in the heavenly realms. Therefore put on the full armor of God, so that when the day of evil comes, you may be able to stand your ground, and after you have done everything, to stand. Stand firm then, with the belt of truth buckled around your waist, with the breastplate of righteousness in place, and with your feet fitted with the readiness that comes from the gospel of peace. In addition to all this, take up the shield of faith, with which you can extinguish all the flaming arrows of the evil one. Take the helmet of salvation and the sword of the Spirit, which is the word of God. Ephesians 6:10-17

Show Me Father,
When My Motives Are Selfish

*Do nothing out of selfish ambition or vain conceit, but in
humility consider others better than yourselves. Each of you
should look not only to your own interests, but also to the
interests of others.* Philippians 2:3-4

You are probably wondering what application this verse has for a
parent. I think its message is applicable to many of us who have
a child with an eating disorder. Typically, a daughter with an eating
disorder is one who is very self-absorbed and the parent is the self-
sacrificing one for her sake. In my case, it certainly appeared as if all
I was doing was for selfless purposes. I was quite surprised when I
more closely examined my motives to find that some were not as
selfless as I thought.

I discovered I had certain needs for significance, security, and
happiness. Sometimes I tried to get these fulfilled through other
people, especially my family. My purpose as a good mother was met
if my daughter was well adjusted and well liked. My happiness could
be achieved as long as there was no family conflict and everyone was
growing spiritually. My need for security was met through knowing
that everything was under control and my children were safe.
During family therapy, I began to see how important it was for me
to get these needs met, and I recognized the patterns of behavior
that would ensure this. Needless to say, I was astonished to discover
that what I was doing was not necessarily a good choice for my family. The irony was that I thought I had everyone's best interest at
heart, when I really had only mine.

One answer to my problem came through a girlfriend who
moved away from her hometown to Alaska when she got married.
Without family and friends, she and her husband celebrated her
birthday without much fanfare. She grew very lonely and melancholy,

feeling neglected and unloved on what should be a special day with friends and relatives giving cards and gifts. Her mood worsened each year to the point that her husband could remember the date by her approaching depression. One year she had a grand idea! She decided to turn her birthday around from a focus on herself to a focus on others; and thus began a tradition of hosting a nice luncheon on her birthday. She selected several dear people to whom she wanted to express gratitude for their friendship or contribution to her life. Needless to say, her depression lifted and has not returned since that day.

I absolutely love this gesture! Rather than being concerned with how she was going to get her needs met, she occupied her day with blessing others. Her example has helped me focus more on others than on myself.

It's A Fine Line

Lord, I'm irritated with my child.
Let's face it, I'm an irritated person who
Irritates others. Now I feel like Job's wife
Instead of Job. You will have to give me
Your patience and endurance, Lord.
I find them in short supply in my spirit
Right now. I've **over-given** if there is
Such a term and now I'm irritated and
Working toward becoming angry. If I were
A battery, and You checked to see
How **good** and irritated I am, I'd rank
Right up there with the **fully-charged.**
I don't know anything to do except
Give these feelings and my child to You.
I don't make her decisions anymore,
Even though I wish I could.
I can only advise and right now I haven't
Been asked. I think I'm getting a taste
Of what You go through all of the time
With us as Your children. Lord, use this
Frustration I feel to make me more sensitive
In my own heart to my relationship with You
As my heavenly Father. Teach me to come
To You for advice and guidance to save me
From unhappiness down the road.
It's a fine line that a parent walks when
Her child is an adult who needs help. Help me
Be a parent who helps within Your will,
And not my own. Help me help my child.

Teach Me to Forgive As You Forgive Me

If your brother sins, rebuke him, and if he repents, forgive him. If he sins against you seven times in a day, and seven times comes back to you and says "I repent," forgive him.
Luke 17:3-4

During family week at Remuda Ranch, my family and I recognized behavior patterns in each of us that needed to change. Most of these patterns involved changes that would enhance communication and relationships. For example, we learned to use "I" statements when addressing each other rather than saying "You did…." During the first few months we all consciously attempted to walk using the new, healthy behaviors. As time passed, we each became more relaxed and subsequently careless, resulting in old patterns of behavior that were disruptive to recovery. I had become especially impatient with my husband, who I felt should have had the greatest responsibility for these changes since he was the spiritual leader of our family.

I finally realized that I needed to re-examine my expectations of him, as well as forgive him. When a person fails, are we not to forgive? Absolutely! This verse says to rebuke him (confront in an appropriate manner), but then quickly extend forgiveness. This is required with each offense, over and over again. I confessed my disappointment with my husband and forgave him. He noticed the difference in my attitude and shared that it made him much more willing to lead by example. Confrontation and forgiveness led to a "win-win" situation for all of us.

A Husband's Love

My wife has an eating disorder that, at times, drives me crazy. There are times I feel I will never be at peace until my wife stops her excessive focus on weight and exercise. I feel enslaved by her obsessions. They not only control her, but also control our relationship. When I feel this way, I also become very angry and judgmental. I think my wife is being selfish and thinking only of herself.

However, if I begin to focus (obsess?) too much on her I will say or do something that I will truly regret and that may wound her deeply. Matthew 12:36 says, *"But I tell you, that men will have to give account on the day of judgment for every careless word they have spoken."* God also tells us in Matthew 7:5 to take the log out of our own eye before we try to take the splinter out of our brother's (or sister's) eye.

So, I redirect my thoughts, focus on myself instead of focusing on her, and question my behavior. Have I prayed consistently for my wife? Is my acceptance of her the rule rather than the exception? Do I keep Christ at the center of our relationship? Have I prayed for wisdom? Have I become obsessed with her obsession? After I answer these questions, I ask God to show me a comparable sin in my life. That way I will have more understanding and will not approach her as a judge, but as a loving husband coming alongside her in support. Slowly, I am learning to love.

Lord, help me to be patient and kind towards my wife. Help me not to envy those who seem to be enjoying tremendous progress and increase in their marriages. Through this trial, Lord, I will experience tremendous progress and increase in my ability to love. Through this I will be made more like You! I praise You Lord for my wife!

Comfort Others As They Walk Your Path

Shadows shift across the face of the mountain as the sun hangs low in the west. Before long, the sky transforms into a watercolor canvas upon which the Painter brushes His pastels. Jagged and irregular are the edges of the mountains, now only silhouettes against the colors of sunset. I quietly observe the Creator's majesty from a swing as I rock on the back porch. It is twilight, that peaceful period of time following the conclusion of normal business and preceding the allurement of the evening lights.

I feel comforted as I reflect on the day. Even the vexations of today seem less tumultuous against the serenity this moment holds. The peace I feel has become very precious to me, especially because of the long struggle with my daughter's eating disorder.

What about you? Do you ever receive comfort such as this? Have you walked a long and difficult path with a loved one who has an eating disorder? If you have, consider reaching out to others who have only begun the strife. Do not be hesitant to give counsel when asked and to share what has been positive in your own experiences. Touch the lives of others who are struggling; they may need just that word of encouragement or that act of love you have to give. No one should walk alone.

Praise be to the God and Father of our Lord Jesus Christ, the Father of compassion and the God of all comfort, who comforts us in all our troubles, so that we can comfort those in any trouble with the comfort we ourselves have received from God. 2 Corinthians 1:3-4

If you or someone you know is struggling
with an eating disorder, please contact Remuda Ranch.
1-800-445-1900
remudaranch.com

Hand in Hand
Order Form

Postal orders: The Remuda Cornerstone Bookstore
48 N Tegvier Street
Wickenburg, AZ 85390

Telephone orders: 1-800-445-1900 ext. 4242

E-mail orders: cornerstone@remudaranch.com

Please send *Hand in Hand* to:

Name: _____

Address: _____

City: _____ State: _____

Zip: _____ Telephone: (_____) _____

Book Price: $9.99

Shipping: $3.00 for the first book and $1.00 for each additional book to cover shipping and handling within US, Canada, and Mexico. International orders add $6.00 for the first book and $2.00 for each additional book.

Or order from:
ACW Press
P.O. Box 110390
Nashville, TN 37222

(800) 931-BOOK

or contact your local bookstore